The Miraculous Tale of the Two Maries

by ROSEMARY WELLS

illustrated by PETRA MATHERS

VIKING

VIKING
Published by Penguin Group
Penguin Young Readers Group, 345 Hudson Street, New York, New York 10014, U.S.A.

Penguin Books Ltd, Registered Offices: 80 Strand, London WC2R 0RL, England

First published in 2006 by Viking, a division of Penguin Young Readers Group

1 3 5 7 9 10 8 6 4 2

LIBRARY OF CONGRESS CATALOGING-IN-PUBLICATION DATA
Wells, Rosemary.
The miraculous tale of the two Maries / by Rosemary Wells ; illustrated by Petra Mathers.
p. cm.
Summary: After perishing in a boating accident, two sixteen-year-old girls,
both named Marie, ask God to allow them to return to earth
where they intervene in the lives of villagers.
ISBN 0-670-05960-9 (hardcover)
[1. Miracles—Fiction. 2. Saintes-Maries (France)—Fiction.
3. France—Fiction.] I. Mathers, Petra, ill. II. Title.
PZ7.W46843Mir 2006
[E]—dc22
2005017743
Manufactured in China
Set in Verona
Book design by Nancy Brennan

FOR PETER LEJACQ
—R.W.

TO MY PARENTS
—P.M.

Author's Note

If you ever go to France, into the sunny south where the horses run wild in the lavender, you will find the tiny town called Saintes-Maries-de-la-Mer. Inside the town church is a wooden boat, and in the boat are two wooden ladies—one in a rose dress and one in blue. Both are called Marie.

Behind the altar, where candles flicker in ruby-red glasses, are pictures of forty miracles. The miracles were all recorded in sudden bunches over a sixty-year period ending around 1900. There was something very honest about these carefully documented paintings. I knew these stories were real. I also knew I had stumbled into evidence of an unsolved mystery.

The official church explanation is as unconvincing as the paintings are real. All the guidebooks say the same thing: These miracles were performed by two Biblical women who were set adrift in a boat two thousand years ago, a thousand miles from the coast of France. I, for one, didn't believe a word of this.

For a long time I sat in the church. In the paintings, I saw ordinary citizens, farmers' wives, and innkeepers. They suffered the accidents and illnesses of their own time. Someone helped them. Someone who loved them. Someone in a fishing barque. My eyes wandered to the wooden boat. The two wooden Maries stared back.

"Who were you?" I asked.

—Rosemary Wells

MARIE AND I were local girls.

    We were best friends, and we both shared the name Marie.

    We knew everyone in our little town.

    Our fathers were fishermen in the *étangs*, which is what they call the big lagoons in the south of France.

All the carefree year long, Marie and I rowed around in our boat
and fished and crabbed. We sang all the songs we knew over and over.
People laughed with us. "*Regardez les deux Maries*," they said.
And we had fun.
In our boat, in the gentle waters, we were safe from harm.

Twice a day, the tide went out as far as the eye could see.

Under the mud was a city of clams. Marie's mother just loved to cook big, fat clams in parsley and garlic. But over the clam beds, the tide could flow in so suddenly that many careless clam diggers before us had been swept out to sea.

Our mothers and fathers had made us promise a hundred times we would not go out that far. We did it anyway.

An incoming storm tide flooded us suddenly.
Waves tossed our boat far under the sea and then suddenly up
again, right up to Heaven. We were only sixteen, Marie and I.

I think that God took pity on us when He saw us at the Gates of Heaven, dripping wet and covered with seaweed, our oars still in our hands.

"So young," He said, "and so foolish!"

"We know," we said.

"It is a tragedy," said God. "But that's the end of that."

Now Marie was the kind of girl who was forever coaxing her mother for one last macaroon or five more minutes before she had to go to sleep.

"*S'il vous plaît*," she asked God in her sweetest voice, "could we have another chance, just one more?"

"Another chance!" said God. "Nobody gets another chance! Particularly if they disobey their parents!"

Marie did not like to take no for an answer.

"Oh, dear," she said, "I can hear my mother and father cry. And Marie's mother and father cry! Not to mention my little sister, Juliette! They are all so poor, and now they are heart-broken as well."

"I can hear the weeping of all the mothers and fathers in the world, young lady," said God with a sigh. He turned His ear downward to hear.

"If we promise to live a life of good deeds? If we cross our hearts and hope to die?" wheedled Marie. "Could we just see our families for five minutes more?"

God did not answer. He seemed to forget all about us.

But of course, God does not forget.

We tiptoed over to the boat and climbed in. "Row," Marie whispered.

"What?" I asked.

"Row!" she whispered louder. "Just row!"

I pulled the oars. Soon we were speeding nicely through the clouds.

"I think He is giving us a chance," said Marie.

I asked, "Are we dead or not?"

"I think we are in between the two worlds," said Marie. "*Entre les deux mondes*."

"What kind of an answer is that, Marie?" I demanded.

"Don't nag, Marie," said my friend. "Let's find some good works to do!"

Boating in the sky was so pleasant. Neither Marie nor I
was hungry or tired. Time itself billowed all around us like
cloud mountains in the sky.

Suddenly Marie stopped her oars and said, *"Écoute!"*
I listened.
"Stop rowing. There is an emergency!" said Marie.
And so we rowed downward as fast and hard as we could. We
stopped just outside the window of our next-door neighbors on
Earth. The DuPrés were farmers. They had a
son, Eugène. I used to babysit for Eugène
DuPré.

Eugène's mother and father knelt on the floor beside their son's crib and prayed. We could see that Eugène was very pale and sick. He was too exhausted to cry. We knew in a flash that he was about to leave his mother and father almost as soon as his tiny, short life had begun.

I don't know what made me do it, but I stepped out of the boat and through the window. I put my hand on Eugène's forehead.

"It's just me, Eugène," I said. "Now open your eyes, and I'll give you a chocolate drop."

Eugène opened his eyes and smiled. His mother and father sank to the floor. "Great saints in Heaven!" they said. "Little Eugène is well again! How can we ever thank you?" they asked.

"Go next door. Tell our mothers and fathers that we are all right and that we love them," said Marie.

"We will!" said Eugène's parents. "We surely will! And we will bring them peaches from our orchard for all the years to come."

Marie and I returned to our boat.

"That was easy," said Marie.

Off we went into the clouds again. A rainbow of colors we had never seen on Earth clung to our oarlocks.

It was not long after that Marie stopped and again said, "*Écoute!*"

I listened. From far away there was a howling sound like a baby wolf in a hollow tunnel.

"*Nous descendons!*" I said this time, and we rowed as fast and hard as we could and stopped the boat just over a well.

We hopped out.

"Who's down in there?" asked Marie, jiggling the bucket rope. "Léon Massel? Is that you? Don't panic. Sit in the bucket. Hold tight! We'll get your papa."

I stayed with Léon and sang him songs so that he would stay calm.

Marie ran into the mill where Pierre Massel was sacking flour for bread. She yelled, "Monsieur Massel! Léon's fallen down the well! Hurry up!"

Léon's father came with a ladder and brought his trembling boy up into the sunlight.

"What can I ever do to thank you?" asked Monsieur Massel.

"Bring a loaf of bread to our mothers and fathers," we said. "And tell them that you saw us and that we love them."

"A hundred loaves of bread!" said Monsieur Massel. "And a hundred after that for as long as they still eat bread."

We did not know it at the time, but this was only the beginning.
The next incident began not with the crying of a child but with the
whinnying of horses. It was dark, nighttime on the shores of France.

"*Écoute!*" I said to Marie.

It was not as easy going down in the dark. Warm winds bounced
our little boat around like rolling waves. There, beneath us, in the city
of Arles, was a familiar-looking barge.

"It's Jacques Papin's coal barge!" said Marie. "My father owes him money for the heat in our house. Look! His horses! The ones that pull the barge along the canal—they have all fallen into the water!"

The poor beasts were struggling in the deep, black canal.

Marie put her hand out and touched the muzzle of a frightened mare.

Within a minute the river quieted, and the horses turned and swam safely ashore.

"Who are you?" said one of the bargemen.

Jacques Papin squinted at us from the deck of the *Papin #3*.

"Saints be praised!" he said. "It is my customer's daughter, Marie, and her little friend from down the street. Can you hear me, Marie?"

"Oh, quite well," Marie answered.

"I will bring both your fathers all the coal they will ever need to keep the kitchen warm," said Jacques Papin.

We went up again. We rowed inside a cloud, shipped our oars against the gunnels, and slept for the first time.

The day after, the next week, the following month, there were so many problems that we needed to attend to in our small town on the earth below.

The winemaker's wife, Suzanne, fell under the wheels of their wagon and was nearly trampled to death by the horses. We got there just in time.

Jean Baptiste, the cheesemonger, was bitten by a starving stray dog. We interceded. Then we found a home for the poor dog where he had enough to eat.

In an old inn at the edge of town, a harvest party was held
for all the farmers from the region. Under their weight, the floor
collapsed. We got there in the nick of time.

Each of our miracles made work for the town artists. These artists painted exactly what people had seen. Rolling barrels, runaway horses, kicking donkeys. And us in our boat in the sky. Marie and I kept the artists busy for many years.

Our parents grew rich with presents from thankful townspeople. They lived long and happy lives. And although they did not see us, they knew we were nearby at all times.

We did not lose our powers until the day came when all our families and neighbors and their children had come to the Gates of Heaven, and the world below our boat was filled with new people.

Someday you may go into the church in our tiny town in the south of France. You will see Eugène in his bed, and Léon coming out of the well in his papa's arms.

Each of our miracles is there, just as it happened.

They will tell you we were grand and famous saints.

But you will know we were just two best friends in a boat who loved all the people in our town.